ISBN
978-1-4828-8045-8 (sc)
978-1-4828-8044-1 (e)

Print information available on the last page.

To order additional copies of this book, contact
Toll Free 800 101 2657 (Singapore)
Toll Free 1 800 81 7340 (Malaysia)
www.partridgepublishing.com/singapore
orders.singapore@partridgepublishing.com

10/06/2016

PARTRIDGE

Freddie takes Daisy for a Walk

Diana S. Duncan

For Daisy

Our Daisy was fond of nice ribbons and bows.

She brushed her hair daily, washed her face so it glowed.

She loved all her lessons, read books night and day,

'til Dad told her kindly, 'Don't just work, also play!'

'Don't care what you look like. Go out and climb trees.

Spend time out with Freddie; *he's* free as the breeze.

You're too keen on homework; you need to chill out.

Skip around in the park. Be a *kid*, run about!'

'Sometimes I feel lonely,' Daisy told him that night.

'Don't worry,' he said. 'We'll soon put that right.

You can have kids for sleepovers, have kids to play.

Learn soccer and netball. You'll make pals that way.'

Now Daisy's dog Freddie was *old- not* a pup.

But Mum always grumbled, 'He just won't grow up!

He's so naughty and wayward, so hard to control.

When I take him out walking, it's a race, not a stroll!'

'Oh, Mum, let *me* walk him,' said Daisy next day.

'I'm stricter than you are; he won't run away.'

On a golden, cool morning in spring, they set out.

'*You* lead,' Mum said sternly, 'or he'll boss you about!'

'Though Daisy pulled hard on his lead and cried, 'Stop,'

Freddie ran like the wind to his favourite shop.

The butcher was waiting and threw him a bone.

'Hi Daisy,' he said. 'Freddie's usually alone.'

'When he calls in to see us, he says thanks with a bark,

then carries his bone down the road to the park.'

Daisy clung to his lead as he dashed everywhere.

She got mud on her sneakers and leaves in her hair!

The sandpit was next. To the children's surprise,

Freddie buried his bone and kicked sand in their eyes.

He flopped on the grass and stretched out in the sun.

Daisy lay down beside him and said, 'This is *fun*!'

'See that cloud up there, Freddie, that looks like a house?

If you screw up your eyes, it looks more like a mouse.'

But Freddie was up now and chasing a cat.

Daisy pulled on his lead, running this way and that.

The next thing she knew, they were down by the stream,

and Freddie jumped in, like a cat with the cream.

He chased all the ducks. How they quacked and complained!

They rose in the sky and looked down with disdain.

Some people cried, 'Hey there. Your dog is a pest.'

But Daisy just waved and called, 'No, he's the best!

He's just a free spirit, and freedom is good.

I'd be more laid-back — like him — if I could.'

Yet Freddie was calm, as good as could be,

when he led Daisy home. It was time for his tea!

'What happened?' said Mum. 'Where have you been?

You look such a mess; go upstairs and get clean.'

'Oh, Mum, that was *awesome*,' Daisy said with a smile.

'Freddie taught me a lesson that was really worthwhile.

And hey, guess what, Dad? We found a café

Where they serve doggie - cinos. Can I walk him each day?'

'You sure can,' said Dad. 'I'm proud as can be.

You've learnt that the best things in life are for free.

Though it's good to try hard and get homework done.

It's also important for you to have fun.'

When Daisy tucked Freddie that night into bed,

'You're my best friend,' she whispered and patted his head.

And Freddie sighed, as he dreamed, under the night sky,

Of huge bones, and slow cats, and ducks that can't fly!

Made in the USA
Middletown, DE
21 July 2017